PLEASE

NO SOLICITING
PEDDLING
Distribution of
PAMPHLETS

Für meine Großeltern
For my grandparents

All rights reserved. Published in the United States by Random House Studio, an imprint of
Random House Children's Books, a division of Penguin Random House LLC,
1745 Broadway, New York, NY 10019.

Random House Studio with colophon is a registered trademark of Penguin Random House LLC.

Visit us on the Web! rhcbooks.com

Educators and librarians, for a variety of teaching tools, visit us at RHTeachersLibrarians.com

Library of Congress Cataloging-in-Publication Data is available upon request.
ISBN 978-0-593-71078-4 (hardcover)
ISBN 978-0-593-71079-1 (lib. bdg.)
ISBN 978-0-593-71080-7 (ebook)

The artist used mixed media to create the illustrations for this book.
The text of this book is set in 16-point Tibere Medium.
Interior design by Paula Baver

MANUFACTURED IN CHINA
10 9 8 7 6 5 4 3 2 1
First Edition

VIVIEN MILDENBERGER

otto
AND THE
story
tree

RANDOM HOUSE STUDIO 🏠 NEW YORK

Otto was a cranky old bird.

He had mottled feathers because he rarely took a bath. "Ack! What's the point?!" he said as he glanced at himself in the mirror.

He lived in the dark because he never
opened the windows.

"Ack! What's the point?!" he said when
he noticed the latches had rusted shut.

He never mopped or dusted because
he never had visitors.

"Ack! What's the point?!" he said as his
tail feathers trailed across the grimy floor.

One day he was preparing his dinner, just as
he did every evening.

"Ack! What's the point?!" he said when a seed
spilled out of his dinner bowl.

As Otto settled into his armchair, he eyed
the little seed on the ground in front of him. . . .

"Oh, little seed, if only you knew . . . You're so small, and the world is so big. I've seen some marvelous things in my day. I once found myself caught in a fierce storm during a hot-air balloon ride, battling the thunder and lightning with nothing but my goggles and wits to guide me."

Eventually, Otto nodded off to sleep.

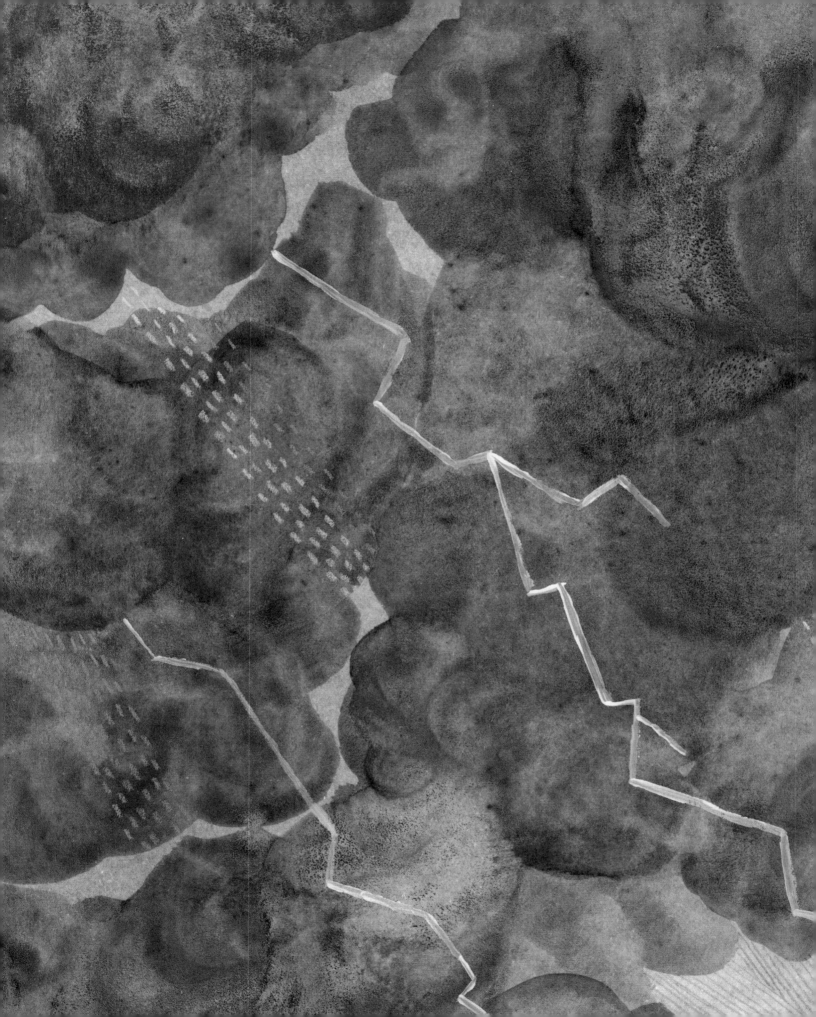

The next morning he awoke to find a sprout
where the seed should have been.

"I'd better pull it out," Otto thought, since
the sprout didn't belong there.

"Ack! What's the point?!" he grumbled
as he went about fixing breakfast.

That evening Otto returned to his
armchair, as he always did after dinner.
He looked down at the sprout.

"Little sprout, if only you knew . . .
I've seen some marvelous things in my
day. I once battled an evil queen with
only a spoon and my trusty tambourine."

And once again Otto told the sprout
of his adventures until he fell asleep.

Each day he told it stories, and each day the sprout

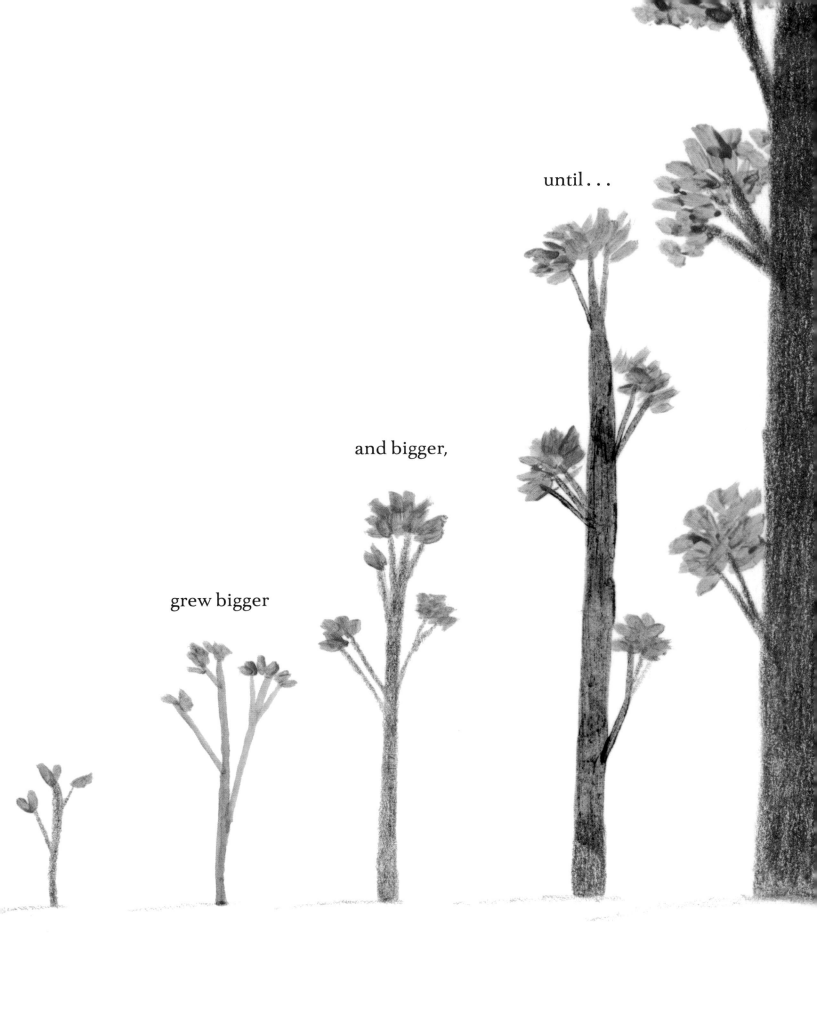

grew bigger

and bigger,

until . . .

. . . one morning Otto awoke to sunlight on his face. He looked up
and found that the sprout had grown into an enormous tree that
had burst through the ceiling. A fresh breeze whistled in through
the cracks in the roof and blew all the dust off the floor. Dew trickled
down onto his forehead and washed his mottled feathers.

He suddenly felt like opening the windows.

That evening Otto settled himself into his armchair, as he did every night.

"Oh, my dear tree, if only you knew . . . I've seen some marvelous things in my day. I once journeyed through the dark forest with nothing but a compass that always pointed in the wrong direction and a lantern that brought shadows to life."

He was halfway through the story when he began to nod off.

Suddenly a little voice from above said, "Oh, please, just five more minutes! I want to know how it ends!"

A little bird had settled on one of the high branches for the night.

"Oh, yes, please! I do too!" another voice chimed in. A spider had started spinning its web between some of the tree's leaves.

Surprised, and with only a little grumble, Otto finished his story.

Each evening more and more animals gathered in the tree's
towering branches, hoping to catch one of Otto's thrilling tales.
Birds settled in for the night after long days of flight. Caterpillars
listened in their chrysalises while they became butterflies.
Spiders wove their webs, and squirrels stashed their acorns.
And each evening the tweeting and scuttling would grow ever
so quiet. It was time for another story.

"Oh, my friends, if only you knew . . . I've seen some marvelous things in my day. . . ."

And so it went, every night. Otto never even thought about patching up the holes in his ceiling.

"Ack! What's the point?!"